For Jonah

SIMON & SCHUSTER BOOKS FOR YOUNG READERS
An imprint of Simon & Schuster Children's Publishing Division
1230 Avenue of the Americas, New York, New York 10020
Copyright © 2016 by Jim LaMarche • All rights reserved, including the
right of reproduction in whole or in part in any form. • SIMON & SCHUSTER
BOOKS FOR YOUNG READERS is a trademark of Simon & Schuster, Inc.
For information about special discounts for bulk purchases, please contact
Simon & Schuster Special Sales at 1-866-506-1949 or business@simonandschuster.com.
The Simon & Schuster Speakers Bureau can bring authors to your live event.
For more information or to book an event, contact the Simon & Schuster Speakers
Bureau at 1-866-248-3049 or visit our website at www.simonspeakers.com.
Book design by Lizzy Bromley • The text for this book was set in Bembo.
The illustrations for this book were rendered in acrylics, colored pencils,
and opaque inks on Arches watercolor paper.
Manufactured in China • 0616 SCP • First Edition
10 9 8 7 6 5 4 3 2 1
Cataloging-in-Publication data for this book is available from the Library of Congress.
ISBN 978-1-4814-4735-5
ISBN 978-1-4814-4736-2 (eBook)

Pond

Jim LaMarche

A PAULA WISEMAN BOOK
Simon & Schuster Books for Young Readers
New York London Toronto Sydney New Delhi

This is so weird," I said to myself as I watched the clear water bubble up from the ground.

We had always called it "the Pit."

I followed the icy stream as it ran through the sand and gravel and passed through the big rocks out into the woods. I slowly looked all around me. "It's not a pit," I said out loud. "I can do it, but I'm going to need help."

I ran home and gathered my sister, Katie, and my best friend, Pablo. "The Pit . . . ," I said excitedly.

"Yeah, so?" said Pablo.

"I think the pit was once a pond!" I said. I told them about the bubbling water and my idea.

"Let's do it, Matt!" said Pablo.

"I'm in," said Katie.

The next Saturday we started early. We gathered up the junk, the old tires, bottles, and rusted cans, and filled our wheelbarrow. Pablo's dad helped us take it all to the dump. Next we started on the new dam. We got big stones and old logs from the woods. Katie kept finding pretty feathers. "I can use these," she said.

The dam took days to finish. One morning as we worked, Pablo yelled, "You've got to see this!"

"It was half buried in the sand!" said Pablo.
"It's beautiful," Katie said as she washed the dirt away.
We all took turns holding and studying the heart stone.
"Do you think somebody made this?" I asked.

The pond filled slowly as the warm spring days passed. Wherever we found a leak we plugged it with more rocks and branches and muddy grasses. As we waited, Pablo practiced his music and Katie read to us about the new birds and bugs we were seeing arrive at the pond. "I think the heart stone is made of quartz," she said one day. "Blue quartz."

As summer arrived so did the bugs and the rainstorms. There were good bugs like the dragonflies and honeybees and horrible bugs like the mosquitoes and nasty horseflies that bit hard and left itchy welts.

The bugs were bad enough, but when the afternoon thunderstorms came, we had to run for home.

Pablo loved the big storms.

"All right, let's get to work!" said Dad.

The day before, we had dragged the old wooden boat into the pond. It had started leaking immediately. At dinner we had told Dad about the boat.

"I can't believe it's still there," he had said quietly. "Let's see what we can do in the morning."

As Dad patched and puttied the holes and cracks, Pablo sanded out the slivers and I nailed down all the loose boards. Katie painted a dragonfly on the bow. "We'll call it the *Dragonfly*," she said.

"The *Dragonfly* floats!" Pablo proclaimed as we pulled the boat into the pond. The water was cool and crystal clear and shallow enough to walk around the entire pond. We all took our turn pulling the boat.

"Those are barn swallows," said Katie. "They eat mosquitoes."

"Well, then, I love barn swallows," said Pablo.

Summer went by too quickly. The last week before school started our dad noticed us moping around. "You need a summer celebration," he said. "I haven't used this gear in years," Dad said as he got the tent and sleeping bags out of the garage.

At the pond we ate hot dogs and drank cocoa and sang corny camp songs, and Katie did what she called her dragonfly dance. We stayed up long past dark and watched as millions of stars came out.

It was late fall when we started hearing the geese. In other years they had always flown in Vs high above us. But now, in the late afternoons, hundreds of them would fly down and rest on our pond. Pablo called it the "Goose Hotel." The geese seemed nervous with us in the boat, but Pablo sang and played his songs softly, and the geese calmed and swam up close to us.

"They're hungry," I said. "Let's get some bread."

"My book says they should only eat the food they find in the wild," said Miss Know-it-all Katie.

It was almost January before the pond froze solid enough to skate on. On some Saturdays we would have skating parties with all our friends. Pablo's mom would bring us big pots of hot chili and cocoa and we would skate all day until the sun set.

The ice on the pond finally melted, and after a long winter of heavy coats and boots, it felt good to run in the warm spring air. "To the top of the mountain!" Pablo yelled as he ran ahead of us up the little hill.

At the top Pablo reached in his pocket and took out the heart stone. "Look at the pond," he said in a whisper as he handed me the stone.

"How come we didn't see it before?" asked Katie.

"We were just too close," I said.

"It belongs in the pond. We should put it back," said Pablo.

"What! That's crazy!" I said.

"Pablo's right. The heart belongs back in the pond," said Katie quietly.

By the time we climbed back down they had convinced me, too. "Yeah, I guess so," I mumbled.

"Pablo, you found it, you should do it," said Katie.

We took turns holding the heart one more time, then Pablo skipped the stone back into the center of the pond. "One skip for each of us," he said.

Something odd happened later that afternoon. As we sat on the bank
and made our summer plans, some of the animals and birds we had
seen the past year gathered around us. Without any noise we watched
one another for a long while, and then slowly they walked or swam
away and went back to their homes. And then we went back to our
homes too.